Peg Leg Peke

by brie spangler

Alfred A. Knopf New York

Hello there!
How are you
today?

Oh my, it looks like your leg is stiff as a board.

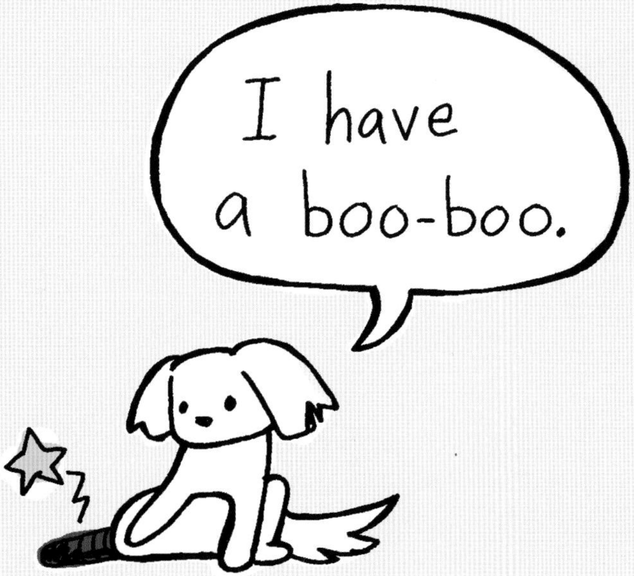
I have a boo-boo.

What

happened?

So it's a cast!
I thought you
were a pirate.

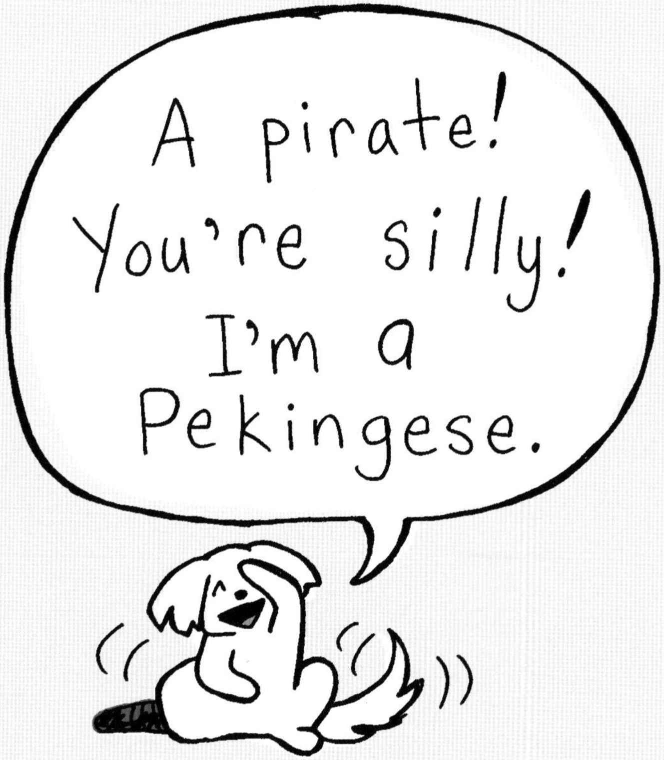
A pirate! You're silly! I'm a Pekingese.

You could be
a pirate.

With a peg leg!

A big hat
with a plume and
a scarf too.

And don't
forget your
eye patch.

You're a great pirate!
I bet you can find something
to make you feel better.

Do you know where to look for your treasure?

East it is!
Let's find your treasure.

East is this way.

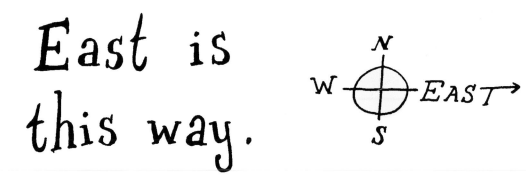

I bet the ✦TREASURE✦
will make you feel better.

Keep going! Remember,
X marks the spot.

That's a lovely
anchor you've got there.

To my family—I love you guys.

THIS IS A BORZOI BOOK PUBLISHED BY ALFRED A. KNOPF

Copyright © 2008 by Brie Spangler

All rights reserved. Published in the United States by Alfred A. Knopf,
an imprint of Random House Children's Books, a division of Random House, Inc., New York.

Knopf, Borzoi Books, and the colophon are registered trademarks of Random House, Inc.

Visit us on the Web! www.randomhouse.com/kids

Educators and librarians, for a variety of teaching tools, visit us at www.randomhouse.com/teachers

Library of Congress Cataloging-in-Publication Data
Spangler, Brie.
Peg Leg Peke / Brie Spangler. — 1st ed.
p. cm.
Summary: When Peke, a Pekingese puppy, breaks his leg, he fantasizes that he is a pirate in search of buried treasure.
ISBN 978-0-375-84888-9 (trade) — ISBN 978-0-375-94888-6 (lib. bdg.)
[1. Pekingese dog—Fiction. 2. Dogs—Fiction. 3. Animals—Infancy—Fiction.
4. Imagination—Fiction. 5. Pirates—Fiction. 6. Buried treasure—Fiction.] I. Title.
PZ7.S7365Pe 2008
[E]—dc22   2007033241

PRINTED IN CHINA

June 2008

10 9 8 7 6 5 4 3 2 1

First Edition